Learning Games

OLD MACDONALD HAD A FARM

This is a great rhyme to sing on the road – children love making the animal noises. With a group of kids, each child can be a different animal.

ONE, TWO, BUCKLE MY SHOE

Help your child learn to count, do up their shoes and increase their dexterity. Encourage them to do the actions in the rhyme – doing up shoes, picking up sticks, and so on. Show them how to count the mice, chicks and other creatures in the story, and chant the rhyme, so children can clap along with it.

ROUND AND ROUND THE GARDEN

A favorite rhyme that is guaranteed to end with giggles! Trace a circle with your finger round and round on your child's palm as you recite the rhyme. "one step, two step" – jump your finger up their arm and tickle them under the arm. Ask them to play the game on your hand!

THIS LITTLE PIG

Toe time! Each toe is a "pig". Starting with your child's big toe, wiggle one toe for each line of the rhyme. Encourage your child to say the words with you and to count their toes as you say the rhyme.

Published 2004 by Tucker Slingsby Ltd

This US edition produced for Borders Group, Inc.

Devised and produced by Tucker Slingsby Ltd
Roebuck House, 288 Upper Richmond Road West
London SW14 7JG, England

Illustrations by Jan Lewis

ISBN 1-902272-32-3

Manufactured in Singapore by Imago

1 2 3 4 5 6 7 8 9 08 07 06 05 04

Color reproduction by Bright Arts Graphics, Singapore

Mother Goose
Action Rhymes

Old MacDonald had a Farm

One, Two, Buckle my Shoe

Round and Round the Garden

This Little Pig

T S

'Old Macdonald had a farm

Ee-aye-ee

aye-oh!

And on that farm

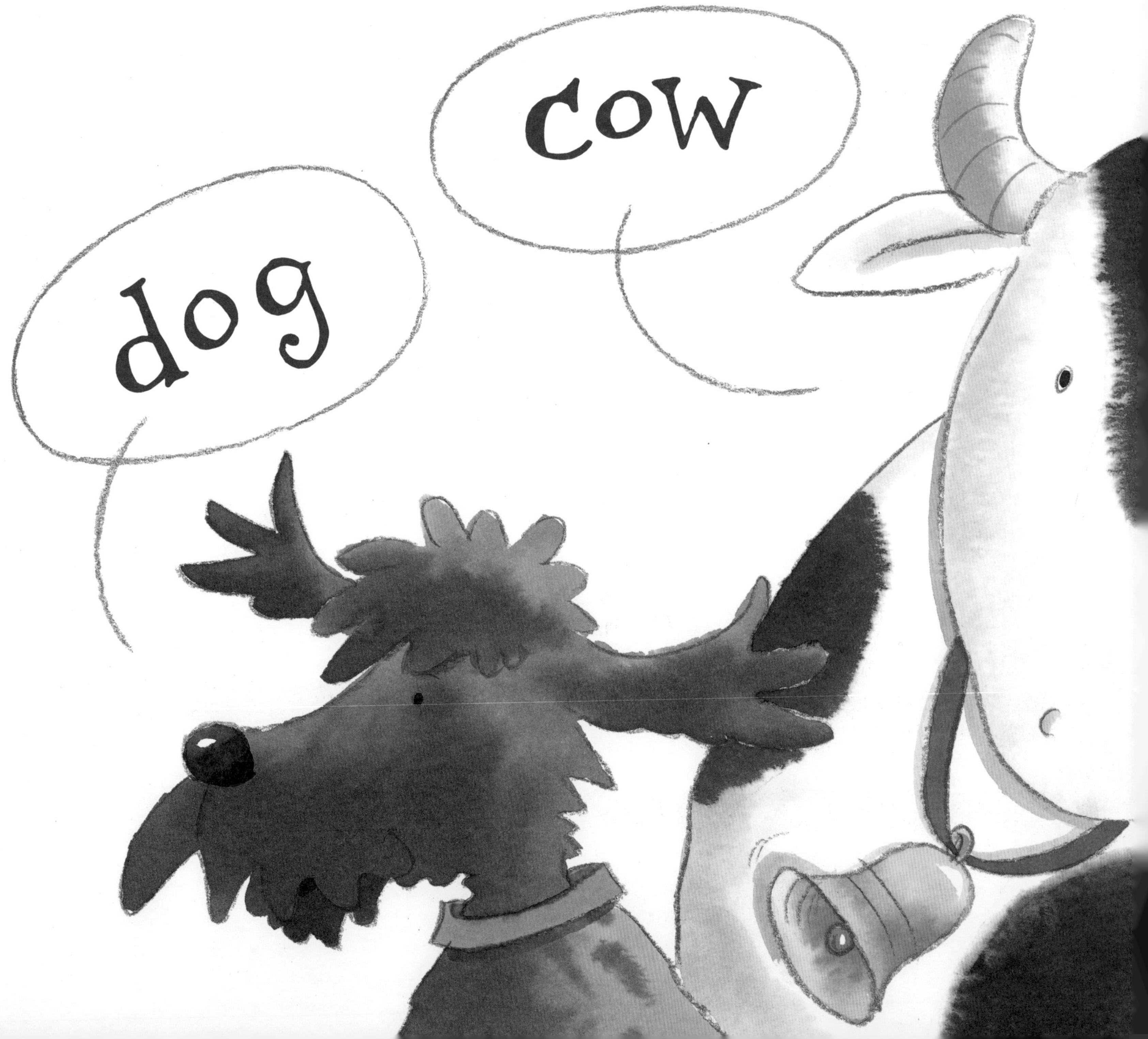

"Ee-aye-ee

aye-oh!

and a

moo
moo

there.

"And a

Woof
Woof

here...

and a

woof
woof

there.

'Here a

baa

there a

baa

'Here a

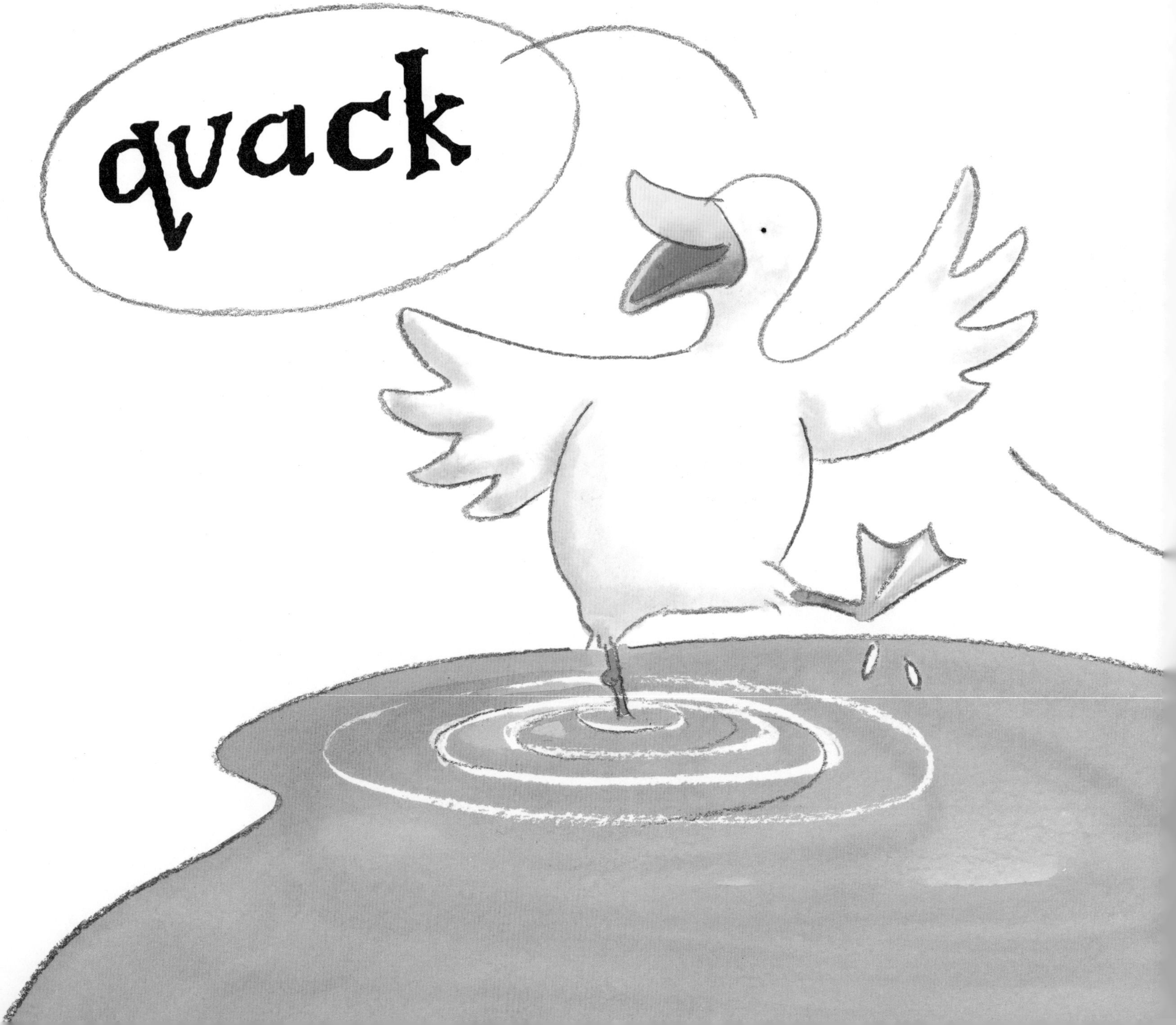

there a quack

Everywhere a

'Old Macdonald
'Ee-aye-ee -

had a farm, aye-oh!

THE END

ONE, TWO, BUCKLE MY SHOE

One

Two

buckle
my
shoe

Three

Four

"Knock at the door.

Five

Six

Pick up
Sticks

Seven

Eight

"Lay them straight"

Nine

Ten

A big fat hen!

THE END

ROUND AND ROUND THE GARDEN

'Round
and
round
the
garden

'Like a

teddy bear.

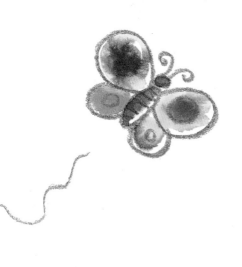

One step

'Two steps

'Tickle you

under there!

"Round
and
round
the
garden

"In the wind and rain.

'One Step

Two steps

'Tickle you there again!

THE END

THIS LITTLE PIG

This little pig

Went to market.

This little pig

stayed
at
home.

This little pig

had roast

beef,

"This little

pig had none.

and this little pig...

...Went ee ee ee eo

all the way home.

THE END